Jack, the Prince of Ireland

by Robert Moulthrop

A SAMUEL FRENCH ACTING EDITION

SAMUEL FRENCH

FOUNDED 1830

SAMUELFRENCH.COM

MUSIC USE NOTE

Licensees are solely responsible for obtaining formal written permission from copyright owners to use copyrighted music in the performance of this play and are strongly cautioned to do so. If no such permission is obtained by the licensee, then the licensee must use only original music that the licensee owns and controls. Licensees are solely responsible and liable for all music clearances and shall indemnify the copyright owners of the play and their licensing agent, Samuel French, Inc., against any costs, expenses, losses and liabilities arising from the use of music by licensees.

IMPORTANT BILLING AND CREDIT REQUIREMENTS

All producers of *JACK, THE PRINCE OF IRELAND must* give credit to the Author of the Play in all programs distributed in connection with performances of the Play, and in all instances in which the title of the Play appears for the purposes of advertising, publicizing or otherwise exploiting the Play and/or a production. The name of the Author *must* appear on a separate line on which no other name appears, immediately following the title and *must* appear in size of type not less than fifty percent of the size of the title type.

JACK, THE PRINCE OF IRELAND was originally produced at Manhattan Children's Theatre in February, 2008. It was directed by Laura Stevens, with set/props/lighting design by Lance Harkins, and stage managed by Christie Love Santiago. The cast was as follows:

JACK . . . . Phil Newsome

BILLY, WISE OLD MAN, DRAGON . . . . Brady Adair

GRISELDA, LEPRECHAUN . . . . Katie Cunningham

TEDDY, DRAGON . . . . .Griffin DuBois

QUEEN MATILDA, BALTHAZAR . . . . Emily Clare Zempel

CHARACTERS

KING OF IRELAND – (voiceover)

BILLY – his eldest son (doubles **WISE OLD MAN, DRAGON**)

TEDDY – his second son (doubles **DRAGON**)

JACK – his youngest son

LEPRECHAUN

WISE OLD MAN

QUEEN MATILDA – (doubles **BALTHAZAR**, the horse)

GRISELDA – her daughter (doubles **LEPRECHAUN**)

QUEEN OF THE GOLDEN MINES – (Voiceover)

BEES – (Audience)

DRAGON – (2 actors)

BALTHAZAR – the horse

AUTHOR'S NOTES

DOUBLING: Doubling above was as for MCT production. Other productions may find other ways to double effectively.

MUSIC: Irish music for dancing, and other kinds of Irish music and other music for sequences such as traveling and battle.

PROPS: The green four leaf clover (and its "turned to gold" counterpart) should be large and solid. The squirrel and the "castle in the distance" can be cutouts on sticks. The rock Jack gets tied to can be a set piece, with its own rope. The BEES can be made from pipecleaners and put on sticks. (They should be given to the children to hold; when they are part of the plot, the children wave them at the characters.)

AUDIENCE PARTICIPATION: There are a number of places to engage the audience directly (i.e., "communicating shamrock") and at least fourplaces where the audience has "lines" they can learn during the warm-up. The lines are
    "Into the Dungeon"
    "Out of the Dungeon"
    "Feet Stop"
    BEES – buzzing and angry; nice and friendly

NARRATION: JACK alternates between his character and telling the story in character.

LAZZI: Bits of business (lazzi) are integral to the piece. Some were written and developed, some were developed during rehearsal and written. Depending on actors and potential audience, there may be other lazzi that will work within the context of the play. Go for it!

(After audience warm-up, house lights out, music up, and JACK steps forward to start the story.)

JACK. Hi. My name is Jack. This story is about me…and how I became the prince of Ireland. My father was the king of Ireland. I was the youngest of three brothers. My older brothers, make no mistake about it, were brave and able boys…and me? Well…I was the youngest. And though they did not think of me as able and brave as them, I did have a way with finding things… *(looks around; finds grass with clover)* What's this? Look at this here. This clover in the grass, why it has four leaves to it, and all the rest of these has only three. I think I have to keep this four leaf clover, because you never ever know when something that's out of the ordinary is going to become a special something.

(TEDDY and BILLY enter.)

TEDDY. Now that I'm grown up, I want to travel and see the world.

BILLY. Me, too. That's what I want to do. See the world.

TEDDY. I said it first.

BILLY. But I thought it first. So I get to be first.

TEDDY. But I'm the smartest.

BILLY. But I'm the oldest.

JACK. And the King said…

KING. *(V.O.)* Begone with the both of youse. You stick around here you'll be driving me crazy. You stay here and you'll be nothing but good-for-nothing omad-hauns, and that's the truth. Out, out, out, the two of youse I say.

JACK. And so they packed up what they thought they might need – a compass, some crackers, and their favorite game of checkers…

*(**BILLY** and **TEDDY** do not react. **JACK** waits a beat, then says…)*

JACK. And so they packed up what they thought they might need…

*(**BILLY** and **TEDDY** react, and begin to pack.)*

BOTH. Mine. It's mine. No, it's mine. No, it's mine. Oh wait, this one's yours. No mine.

(They fight over the checkers, drop the board and pieces, say together…)

Now look what you did!

(…continue squabble while packing, as…)

KING. *(V.O.)* And this boy, this goonie gormless fellow, this youngest son of mine, he seems good enough for sweeping the stable and chopping the wood. So he can stay.

JACK. And so Billy and Teddy went along.

*(Music up as **BILLY** and **TEDDY** begin journey, starting in one direction, starting over, tripping over their own feet, etc. Music out.)*

But by the end of the first day they were a little tired…

*(**BILLY** and **TEDDY** try to outdo each other with bigger and bigger yawns.)*

…so they laid down, and without even eating a cracker or building a fire or playing a game of checkers, they fell asleep.

*(**BILLY** and **TEDDY** lay down on the ground to sleep; they toss and turn, finally sleep, one of them with extra loud and silly snoring.)*

…But in the middle of the night, they awoke with a start…

TEDDY. Who's there?

BILLY. Wha?? What's going on?

TEDDY. Someone's there, I can tell. I can feel it in my bones. Can't you feel it in your bones?

BILLY. (*feels his bones*) No.

TEDDY. Well, there's something there, as sure as eggs is eggs.

BILLY. Well, tell him to go away, I'm sleepy.

TEDDY. No, you tell him.

BILLY. No, you.

TEDDY. No, you.

BILLY. No, you.

(*Both are quiet and scared for a moment, then…*)

JACK. Hey there!

(**BILLY** *and* **TEDDY** *scream, scare each other, look at each other, scream at the sight of each other, see* **JACK,** *and scream again.*)

JACK. It's only me.

BILLY. What are you doing here?

JACK. Well, see, it's like this. I commenced to think long when I found you both, my beloved brothers, gone and not there. And I sat around for a while with nothing to do, and got myself so lonesome that I couldn't stay behind. And I know that you don't think so much of me, but there I was, and so I says to myself, "Self," says I…

"Well, I may be this and I may be that

But as sure as I'm wearing my green hat

I know I'm Irish and that's a fact

And we always go forward, we never go back!"

So here I am.

TEDDY. Look at you, in clothes not fit for a beggar person, and that silly green hat. You're a king's son and I'm ashamed to be seen with you.

BILLY. Look at what we're wearing. Fit for a king, right?

TEDDY. I don't care if he is our brother, there's not a way in the world we can be seen with him.

BILLY. Not a way, not a whit.

TEDDY. So I say, Be off with you!

BILLY. No, I say, Be off with you! *(look)* We both say

BILLY & TEDDY. Be off. Go one with you. Away, away. *(etc.)*

JACK. I get it, I get it. Okay okay okay. I'm an outcast to you both. And I'm sorry. But we're brothers and all, so I'm coming, no matter what you say.

BILLY & TEDDY. *(look).* Oh yeah?

> *(***JACK*** *is quickly resigned to being tied to a rock, again, the way his brothers always do with him. He stands quietly as they go this way and that, trying to remember how to tie him up, tangling themselves in the rope; at one point* ***TEDDY*** *is spun offstage. They finally tie him to the rock.)*

TEDDY. There. That'll keep him. Wearin' rags and tryin' to spoil our adventure. Bad cess to him for the forlorn creature that he is.

BILLY. Right. Bad cess to him. Phooey!!

> *(***JACK*** *moves, with his rock and rope, to the side of the stage, as the brothers move a small mountain to the center, one they will climb back and forth during the following sequence.)*

JACK. And so they left me there, and they went along and they went along…AND they went along, they were laughing and cracking jokes and telling riddles to each other

BILLY. What goes "Ha! Ha! Ha! Plop!"

TEDDY. Ha ha ha plop. Ha ha ha plop. Ha ha…I don't know. What goes "Ha ha ha plop!"

BILLY. Someone laughing his head off.Get it? Ha…Plop!!

TEDDY. I get it, I get it. It's not so funny, but I get it. Okay, then. Here's one for you. "Why do you always walk with your right foot first?"

BILLY. But I don't. Sometimes I walk like this *(pantomimes)*, and sometimes I walk like this *(pantomimes)*. You know me, it's never the same on any one day or any two taken together.

TEDDY. I repeat, "Why do you always walk with your right foot first?"

BILLY. Oh, it's a riddle, is it? *(pantomimes, or not)* Okay, I give up.

TEDDY. You sure? You sure you give up? You're sure. And you won't be mad when I tell you? Promise?

BILLY. Yeah, yeah, yeah. I promise.

TEDDY. Because when you put one foot forward the other is always left behind! Get it? LEFT…be-hind!

BILLY. I don't get it.

TEDDY. LEFT…be-hind. Doesn't matter which foot, you great goat, one's always in front of the other, and the other's always left behind.

BILLY. But it's my right…

TEDDY. Don't…say…another…word. Anyway, we're almost here.

JACK. And where they were was close enough to the castle of the Queen of the Far Country that they could see it, shining there in the distance, like silver clouds in a bright blue sky.

TEDDY. Come on. Let's go!!

JACK. In the meantime, here I was, tied to my rock. Again.

(*A squirrel bounds in.* **JACK** *makes squirrel noises to get the animal to come to his hand.*)

Here squirrel, here squirrel. Just chew a bit of this rope here and I'll be your friend for life…Aw, nuts!!Not even a squirrel will come near me.

WISE MAN. *(appears)* Was it a squirrel you was wanting? I specializes in squirrels.

JACK. It wasn't actually a squirrel I was thinking about, more their lovely little teeth, you know.

WISE MAN. Their teeth, is it? And what would you be doing wanting with the teeth of a squirrel?

JACK. Well, if I could get those teeth around this rope, and the squirrels and their teeth was to like me enough to give it a chaw or two, then I'd be free of this rock and could get on to see my brothers.

WISE MAN. Free it is that your wanting? And what is it that you and your brothers are up to?

JACK. They're off on the road to see the world and have adventures. And I want to have adventures, too.

> For I may be this and I may be that
>
> But as sure as I'm wearing my green hat
>
> I know I'm Irish and that's a fact
>
> And we always go forward, we never go back!

But if I'm sitting here, tied to this rock, I can't go any-where, and it's making me sure nervous enough to make a cat cry.

WISE MAN. Well, we can't have that, then, can we? You wouldn't happen to have a shamrock about your person, now would you?

JACK. You mean a wondrous green clover with four leaves instead of the three that all the rest have?

WISE MAN. That's exactly what I mean. They're very lucky, you know.

JACK. You couldn't tell it by me. Here. I've had this sham-rock since I was a wee lad I thought is was something special, something out of the ordinary , and all it ever got me was tied to a rock by my two older brothers.

WISE MAN. By the fact that you have one – and a fine sham-rock it is – I can tell you're a young man who opens his eyes. But what I think you need is something a little more, something to help you get your heart's desire, and a little bit more.

JACK. But what's a heart's desire? I don't think I have one of those.

WISE MAN. It's when you know the next thing you want is the absolutely right and only thing in the world that will make you – and someone else – really, really happy.

JACK. No, I don't have that.

WISE MAN. You will, my boy. And when you do, I have no doubt but that you'll be needing this. *(Pulls out the shamrock, it has turned to gold.)*

JACK. Oh my goodness! But I can't take that.

WISE MAN. Not only *can* you take it, you *will* take it. And you'll take this, too *(Hands Jack the stick he's been using as a cane.)*

JACK. But I don't need it. And I can't take your stick. Let's stop a minute. You're right here, and you can untie me, and then I'll find my brothers, and everything will be all right.

WISE MAN. Me boy, the trouble with you is, you don't know what you want and you don't know what you need. Trust me. There's a future for you where you will need this golden shamrock, and another place where you'll need this stick, and when you do, you'll know it, and you will thank me for it. You may need it to find a Leprechaun when you need one.

*(Music up. **LEPRECHAUN** dances across the back. Music out.)*

Or perhaps you'll need a sword.

JACK. A sword? A Leprechaun?

WISE MAN. A little man who sometimes knows just what to do next.

JACK. All right.

WISE MAN. And maybe there will be sometime when you need a horse, and you'll remember you have the shamrock.

*(Music up. **BALTHAZAR** crosses in back.)*

JACK. I could see needing a horse, that's for sure.

WISE MAN. Or when magic bees are buzzing round your head. I'll bet a golden shamrock will be just the ticket.

*(Enter **LEPRECHAUN** with **BEES**, cues audience to be Angry Buzzing Bees.)*

JACK. Magic buzzing bees.

*(**BEES** stop; **LEPRECHAUN** exits.)*

WISE MAN. Or a dragon Just keep it close, and use it quiet. Anyone else touches it, it's back to green it is and gone in a flash.

JACK. Well, if you say so. Thank you. Now if you'll untie me, I'll take my new golden shamrock and my nice strong stick and head off to see my brothers and have adventures.

WISE MAN. *(untying)* I'll do better than that. Just take the next turning to the left, then follow the path to the castle. When you're there, tell the Queen that you're there to meet her daughter, and she'll be pleased, I can tell you.

JACK. So I listened to the old man and went off to the shortcut to the castle. And my brothers, who had no knowledge of shortcuts and only knew they liked to riddle each other and everyone else who came along,…

(BILLY and TEDDY enter, talking. They do not see JACK…)

TEDDY. How do you know if a…

BILLY. No, it's my turn. Knock knock…

TEDDY. I'm not answering any knock knock, because you're not playing fair…

JACK. Where have you been?

(BILLY and TEDDY jump, startled. They see JACK, scream.)

JACK. I've been waiting and waiting. The Queen's been waiting and waiting, too. She says she wants to see the three of us, all together.

TEDDY. Did you say we were your brothers?

BILLY. I hope you didn't tell her that we were your brothers. We don't want anything to do with the likes of you, scruffy and scrawny and wearing rags, a poor soul who won't even stay tied to a giant rock.

TEDDY. So never ever ever say that you and we are brothers. Understand?

JACK. We're not brothers.

TEDDY. Right. Never. Ever.

JACK. Not in any case or any cause or any reason?

BILLY. Not for any case or any cause or any reason, or any wherewithal or anything at all.

JACK. Well, in that case, all right then. I'll just be here and be mum, zip my lip, and brothers have I none.

QUEEN. *(enters)* Welcome, weary travelers. Whence come you and what do you look for in this land of the Far Country?

BILLY. Well, you majesty...

TEDDY. Your gracious majesty.

BILLY. Your gracious majesty...

TEDDY. Tell her a riddle, the one about the feet. Smooth the way, open the doors. People always like a good riddle.

BILLY. What?

TEDDY. About the feet? Tell her that one, she'll love it for sure and we'll get stuffed goose for dinner and maybe she'll let us talk with her daughter.

BILLY. Would it be like, your majesty, that you'd be after hearing a riddle? For I have a couple of fine riddles and my brother here, he seems to think it would be a good way to walk toward a stuffed goose for dinner.

QUEEN. I have no use for riddles, you saucy fellow.

BILLY. But this is a fine riddle, your Majesty. What did one toe say to the other toe?

QUEEN. Toe! Are you speaking of my feet, young man? Who gave you permission to speak about the Royal Foot?

TEDDY. No, your Graciousness. It's just a wee riddle, like enough to make you laugh with the answer. If you don't like toes, well, there's one about an elbow. What did the elbow say when he touched the ear?

BILLY. See, your Royality. Try it? See, bring your elbow up to your ear, here.

TEDDY. Watch me. See? See? It can't be done.

BILLY. So, what did the ear say to the elbow?

TEDDY. I've never even heard of you before! Do you often come to these parts!!! Get it? These parts? The elbow!! The ear!!!

(Silence. Pause. The **BROTHERS** *look at the* **QUEEN,** *at each other, back to the* **QUEEN.** *)*

QUEEN. Do you know that whomever even tries to tell me a riddle I throw them in jail, into my darkest dungeon where the water drips and drips from the sagging walls.

BILLY. Well, then, it wouldn't be me, because I was talking about a tiddle.

QUEEN. A tiddle?.

TEDDY. It's a kind of a way with your feet, like this, a sort of dance where…Well, let me show you. *(Begins to dance a jig.)*

QUEEN. *(to* **JACK***)* Are you related to either of these two?

JACK. *(shakes his head)*

QUEEN. You're not, by any chance, brothers, are you? Because, if you were, well, you seem to have some sense, not a riddling person at all, and if you were related, well then, I might reconsider putting them into a dungeon.

JACK. Well, I'm not anything to them. That's what they always tell me.

BILLY. Tell her.

TEDDY. Tell her, Jack, o brother, o best of brothers.

JACK. I'm not. Like you fellows said. I'm nothing to you and you're nothing to me. Not a thing.

BILLY & TEDDY. JACK…!!!

JACK. No, ma'am, not at all at all.

TEDDY. He's funning again, aren't you, boy-o.

BILLY. Just havin a bit of fun.

TEDDY. Why we've known each other since we was all wee babies, the three of us….

BILLY. and lost our mother…

TEDDY. and our father tried to raise us the best he could, and tell her,

BILLY & TEDDY. ya great ninny, how we're your brothers and we're all brothers the three of us.

JACK. *(shakes his head)* No.

QUEEN. Well, the three of you. I think I need the ones who asked me that terrible riddle to go away. Children!! Tell them to go away! Shoo! Just get into the dungeon for a while and think about your riddles. *(to audience)* Help me, children. We need to send these men to the dungeon. Into the dungeon.

(Audience says; "Into the dungeon, into the dungeon" as **TEDDY** *and* **BILLY** *are whisked off by invisible guards.)*

QUEEN. And you, the other one, Mr. Didn't Ask Me A Riddle…

JACK. Jack's my name.

QUEEN. Right, Jack.

JACK. Jack's my name and Fortune's my fame
And I'll find my way in the world
With a magic shamrock a way to the gold
And all the adventures a man can hold.

QUEEN. Is that right? How interesting. You know, perhaps there's a way you can be useful to me.

JACK. Is that right? Are you going to tell me?

QUEEN. Is that a riddle? You know how I feel about riddles.

JACK. Never a riddle in all the world. Can't abide the things myself. Give me a headache the riddles do.

QUEEN. Good. We'll have a little party to celebrate that you're here and that you can help me.

JACK. A party?

QUEEN. Yes.

(Music up as **BILLY** *and* **TEDDY** *cross upstage, as party guests, wearing silly hats, dancing, and drinking.)*

We'll have dancing with jigs and three rounds of soda bread with sparkling dandelion wine and I'll watch you dance with my daughter.

*(***BILLY** *and* **TEDDY** *exit. Music out.)*

JACK. Your daughter?

QUEEN. Yes. My daughter.

JACK. Well, that's swell, really. That's capital. When's this party now?

QUEEN. In an hour. Yes, an hour. I have to tell the musicians, and the cook needs to pick the dandelions for the wine. Ow Griselda! *(exits)*

JACK. An hour, that's good. Because I need time to learn to dance.

QUEEN. *(enters quickly)* You don't know how to dance? You better learn to dance, young man. *(Pause. Look.)* Dungeon. Deep and dark. Dangerous and Dripping. Damp. Full of things that are very un-dry.

JACK. Un-dry?

QUEEN. Fungus. Mushrooms. Toads. Mil-drew.

(TEDDY, waving a frog, chases BILLY across the back of the stage.)

JACK. Toads?

QUEEN. With warts.

(BILLY and TEDDY enter upstage, dressed as prisoners. They listen and comment.)

BILLY & TEDDY. Warts?

QUEEN. And slime.

BILLY & TEDDY. EW !!!! *(They exit.)*

JACK. I'm not so grand about toads, your Royalness. I've always had a thing about warts, you see, and when my mother was little, I mean, when I was little, my mother would always…

QUEEN. We need not speak of littleness and mothers. I am speaking of Damp. And Toads.

(BILLY and TEDDY offstage loudly say "Ribbit, Ribbit.")

JACK. Yes, your High-And-Mightiness.

QUEEN. So, then. Dancing it is. Right? In an hour. See you then.

JACK. Yes. Sure. Dancing. An hour. What now? *(feels in his pocket. Takes out the shamrock, now gold.)* Here. What's this? Sure and this is from that Wise Man, a shamrock turned to gold…that's supposed to be magical!!! But what kind of magic? Hello, Shamrock? Are you listening? Can you talk?

*(*JACK *holds the shamrock up to his ear, hears nothing. Holds it out to an audience member, puts it to his/her ear.)*

Can you hear anything? Is it speaking to you?

*(*JACK *shakes his head in sympathy. Then he tries talking into the shamrock as if it were a phone.)*

Hello! Hello! Jack here. Anyone there at the other end of the shamrock? Hello?…All right, it doesn't talk and it doesn't listen. Not what you might call a communicatin' shamrock.

Maybe…maybe it's a wishing shamrock. I wish I had a pot of gold and a mound of hot griddle cakes and soda bread with gobs of melty butter just oozing down. *(looks around)* Nothing there either.

Okay, magic shamrock…you don't talk and you don't give wishes. What kind of magic is it that you do?

WISE MAN *(offstage)* The trouble with you boy is that you don't know what you want and you don't know what you need…

JACK. Need? *(holds shamrock)* I NEED SOMEONE TO TEACH ME TO DANCE…and NOW!!!

LEPRECHAUN. *(appears)* You called?

JACK. I did? I mean, I did, I did. Finally. Yes, I did. I need to know how to dance.

LEPRECHAUN. I'll say. I've never seen such jumping about in all my born days. That kind of jumping, you see, is what you need if you're going to be in a game of hopping or leaping, and even then, well…

JACK. I know, I know. I'm hopeless. My brothers are always telling me I have two left feet.

LEPRECHAUN. Two left feet is it? Why I know a man who would pay money to have two left feet. He has two right feet. Walks like this. *(silly walk)*

JACK. Should I go to him, trade with him? I need to know how to dance, you see. Otherwise I'm for it.

LEPRECHAUN. For what?

JACK. The Dungeon. The Queen told me,

LEPRECHAUN. Well, then. Dancing for the Queen. That's something special, that is. Let's just see if we can't do something about that. First of all, the left and right thing about the feet, I've got a cure for that here. *(takes his cane)* Just a tap of my stick, on your feet and then quick, you'll be dancing as if, you've been prancing for years

(Music. Taps Jack's feet. They start to move, a little bit. Taps again. More movement. Taps again. Feet are out of control.)

LEPRECHAUN. Whoa there! Whoa! Stop that dancing.

JACK. I can't. They won't let me.

LEPRECHAUN. Just speak to them, me boy.

JACK. *(lamely)* Oh, feet, dear feet, please stop. *(dancing continues)*

LEPRECHAUN. You call that speaking? I've heard babies say "Dada" better than that. Speak, man!

JACK. *(strong, but not strong enough)* Feet, stop now *(dancing continues)* Please.

LEPRECHAUN. I think we need some help. *(to audience)* Let's help Jack before he runs out of wind. Help me now. Say "Feet Stop!" Ready?

ALL. FEET STOP!!

(Music out and JACK stops dancing.)

JACK. Whew!

LEPRECHAUN. Very nicely done. I thank you kindly. And so does Jack.

JACK. Oh, yes. Thank you. *(to LEPRECHAUN)* Now what?

LEPRECHAUN. Well, now we get started. How much dancing have you done in the past?

JACK. None.

LEPRECHAUN. Not a step? Not a bit of a step? Never part of a reel? How about this? Ever do this? No. Well then, how about this one? Ever do that? No. My my, you are a hard case. Show me something then, just anything.

(JACK tries, trips, falls, can't do anything.)

JACK. It's no use. I'll never learn to dance. I might as well just go straight to the dungeon.

LEPRECHAUN. But then you'll miss the dance, you'll miss the chance to meet the girl and perhaps perhaps perhaps change your life as now you know it. So. Pick yourself up, dust yourself off, *(LEPRECHAUN blows dust on JACK.)* and start all over again. There, that's better. Now, let's try again.

JACK. That dust there, that wouldn't be magic dust, would it?

LEPRECHAUN. You want it to be magic dust? Well then…

(Music up. They dance, and JACK is able to dance fairly well.)

LEPRECHAUN. You'll not be needing me any more, I'm thinking.

JACK. Well, maybe not about this. *(demos dance)* But what if something else comes along?

LEPRECHAUN. What else could come along that a fine strapping lad like yourself would be needing the help of a poor small insignificant wee auld man like me?

JACK. Well, what if I have to get to a castle, and it's very far away and up a steep mountain and across a bridge…

LEPRECHAUN. Well, then, me boy, we'll cross that bridge when we come to it. No point in trying to cross the bridge now, cause it isn't here, is it?

JACK. Uh, no. No bridge.

(LEPRECHAUN begins to exit.)

JACK. But what if there's a ferocious dragon? With smoke belching from his nostrils…

LEPRECHAUN. *(turns back)* If that's the case, well, we'll cross that dragon when we come to it.

JACK. You'll be there? With me?

LEPRECHAUN. Close as your coat, near as your fingers ends. Just a whisper away. *(as exit)*…away…away

QUEEN. *(enters)* Are you talking to me, Jack? Now, young man, you may take me in to dinner. I hope you have your dancing shoes on, because I've decided I want to dance, too.

JACK. Oh yes, shoes and all. A little dusty but right there. And your daughter?

QUEEN. My daughter? Griselda? Why she's right here, aren't you, dear?

GRISELDA. Yes, Mama. *(accent on the second syllable)*

QUEEN. And you want to dance, don't you dear.

GRISELDA. Yes, Mama.

QUEEN. *(to JACK)* There, I told you. Now you will have *two* dancing partners. And we will keep you hopping, that's for sure.

(*Music.* JACK *dances first with the* QUEEN, *then with the* GRISELDA. *While dancing with the* GRISELDA, *she and* JACK *flirt. The* QUEEN *cuts in to stop the flirting.*)

JACK. Now, your Royal Greatness, I'm hoping that I can ask a favor.

QUEEN. Well?

JACK. It seems that my brothers are still in the dungeon.

QUEEN. Yes. They were very rude with their riddles.

JACK. But now that we've feasted and danced, and they've missed it all, and a wonderful party it was and I thank you for it.

QUEEN. You're welcome. You are very polite.

JACK. You're very welcome.

QUEEN. No, you're welcome.

JACK. No, you're welcome.

QUEEN. I am the Queen, and I get to say who is welcome and who is not. And you, my boy, are welcome. Is that understood?

JACK. Yes, your Elevated Loftiness.

QUEEN. Very well.

JACK. As I was saying, about my brothers…

QUEEN. Yes. They are in the dungeon.

JACK. Well, do you think we could let them out?

QUEEN. Well…on one condition. *(starts to cry)*.

GRISELDA. Oh, Mama, don't cry. *(to JACK)* See, you're upsetting her.

JACK. But I didn't say a thing.

GRISELDA. It's because of your brothers.

JACK. They didn't say anything. They're in the dungeon.

QUEEN. *(through her sobs)*. It's because, because, because… you are all boys, the three of you. And, and, and… *(sobs again)*

JACK. But I can't help it, being a boy. Neither can my brothers. It's who we are, you see.

QUEEN. It isn't that. Its…it's…it's… My own baby boy was stolen, you see.

GRISELDA. It's true. My baby brother.

JACK. Stolen.

QUEEN. Yes. By the Queen of the Golden Mines.

JACK. The Golden Mines?

QUEEN. She's rich, rich as Croesus, rich as the gods of the sun and the moon, rich beyond the telling.

JACK. Got a lot, has she?

QUEEN. But she had no children. And even with all her riches, she knew that a baby boy was all she wanted.

GRISELDA. So one night she sent her army of flying bees and they came to our castle…

QUEEN. And carried away my darling baby boy. My only son. My joy…Not that you aren't wonderful, my darling Griselda.

GRISELDA. Thank you, Mama.

QUEEN. But a mother needs her son. And a son needs his mother. Especially when he's only… *(sob)* …a baby.

JACK. I understand. Truly I do. I was a baby once myself, you know. *(to **GRISELDA**)* Hard to believe, I know, but true it is, nonetheless.

QUEEN. And while you might do nicely, even though your brothers tell those awful riddles, it's not quite the same.

JACK. No, it isn't.

QUEEN. So, if you would go to the Queen of the Golden Mines and get my baby…

JACK. By myself? Well, yes, I can. Be this and be that, I'm no the man to leave you in your trouble if I can help it, and be this and be that all over again, I won't sleep two nights in the same bed nor eat two meals in one house til I find out the golden castle of the Queen of the Golden Mines, and fetch back your darling baby boy to you…or else I'll not come back alive.

QUEEN. Well, that's what I mean. You need some help, I think. You could take your brothers along. They're strong. They could help. You'll need all the help you can get, you see.

GRISELDA. You will.

QUEEN. Don't interrupt. Where was I?

GRISELDA. About needing help…with the Queen…of the Golden Mines…because…

QUEEN. Oh, yes, of course. Because ninety nine men have tried and none have ever succeeded.

JACK. Well, I'll be one hundred to try then, and I'll not turn back without bringing your baby boy.

QUEEN. Her castle sits on the top of the Golden Mountain whose sides are steep

JACK. I'll use a pickax and rope, and climb right up.

QUEEN. And because the mountain is made of gold, it flashes blinding light when sunlight or moonlight bounces against it.

JACK. I'll close my eyes. But climb straight and true nevertheless.

QUEEN. Then there are her magic bees. They make her golden honey. And they use their stingers on whomever approaches the Golden Mountain.

JACK. That must hurt.

QUEEN. Not at all. Their stingers just put you to sleep and turn you into a golden statue.

JACK. Oh, well… No. I don't want that. I'll get by them by wearing a special bee-keeping suit.

GRISELDA. The last 10 tried that. The bees found holes. They're golden statues now.

JACK. Well, what I say is, always keep a positive attitude. I'll find a way to make my suit entirely bee proof.

GRISELDA. Well, I wish you well.

QUEEN. And then there's the dragon.

JACK. The dragon. Does he have smoke coming out of his nose?

GRISELDA. Oh, yes.

JACK. And is there fire belching out of his mouth?

QUEEN. With great regularity, yes.

JACK. I see. Well, in that case…(*Pulls out his sword/stick. He's committed to the quest.*)

(**GRISELDA** *kisses* **JACK** *on the cheek and runs off.*)

QUEEN. Now get along with you and take your brothers with you. You'll need all the help you can get.

JACK. Hey, you two. Out of the dungeon. (to audience) Can I have some help here? Let's get them out of the dungeon. On three. One. Two. Three.

(*With* **JACK**, *audience says: "Out of the dungeon."* **BILLY** *and* **TEDDY** *appear.*)

(to **BILLY** *and* **TEDDY**) We've got an adventure to have here, and a fine one it looks to be. Now, no more riddles while we're on our adventure, cause my brain can't stand the strain of questions and adventure at the same time.

BILLY & TEDDY. Well, all right. If we must, we must.

JACK. For we may be this and we may be that
But as sure as I'm wearing my green hat
We know we're Irish and that's a fact
And we always go forward, we never go back!

BILLY. Always forward and never back!

TEDDY. But where is it exactly that we're going?

JACK. We're off to the castle of the Queen of the Golden Mines to search out the other Queen's baby and bring him back to her.

BILLY. And is this just a regular adventure, like? Where we walk along and knock on the door and say, nice and polite, "Excuse me, Madam Queen of the Golden Mines, can we have the baby back?" And she says, "Why, yes, of course you may," and then we take the baby and come back? Is it that sort of adventure?

JACK. No.

TEDDY. I knew it, I knew it, I knew it. There's a catch, isn't there. That's just like you, Jack. If it isn't one thing, it's always something else, and the other thing is never, ever a good thing, and that's for sure.

JACK. It's nothing, really. Not really anything to worry yourselves about. It's just that, well, the sides of her mountain are made of gold and they're steep and slick as glass.

BILLY. I knew it. A steep mountain. And us with not even a horse.

JACK. And then there's the Golden Bees. With stingers that turn you to golden statues.

TEDDY. Buzzing bees coming at us from all sides, ready to put in their deadly stingers, and us without any protection at all.

JACK. And a dragon.

BILLY. A dragon?

JACK. Yep. Breathing fire and all, with smoke coming out of his nostrils.

TEDDY. What do you think, Billy? That dungeon, it wasn't
so damp after all, and bread and water...

BILLY. Three times a week, fairly generous.

TEDDY. We could go back.

JACK. But fellows. Look. *(takes out golden shamrock)* I've got a
magic shamrock here. It's worked for me once already.
I know it's good for some more. Come on, Billy. Come
on, Teddy. Stick with me. The magic will work, and
we'll have an adventure.

BILLY. Well...

JACK. So we went along . . and we went along, until it was
night, and we went to sleep. At least I went to sleep.

*(JACK sleeps. TEDDY and BILLY pretend to sleep. Check
to see whether JACK is really asleep. Then...)*

TEDDY. I say we just take that magic shamrock now and we
done with it.

BILLY. Shhh! You'll wake the lad.... And I say we wait. He's
said it's a magic shamrock and it looks like a magic shamrock, but the truth is, we've never seen a bit of magic
come out of it at all. What if it's all a bunk and a bevil?

TEDDY. Maybe you're right.

BILLY. So we'll just stick along and be around and by his side
and when we see whether or not it's a real magic shamrock, why then we'll pick him up and tie him down...

TEDDY. To a rock, like last time, only bigger...

BILLY. And we'll have the shamrock and make it make us
rich. We'll have riches enough that we won't need
adventures.

(BILLY and TEDDY sleep.)

JACK. *(wakes)* What a beautiful morning. A clear blue sky
and good fresh air. But now that we're closer to that
Golden Mountain, I'm thinking that a great horse
would be just the thing to help with the climb up the
steep and slippery sides of the mountain. *(takes out
Golden Shamrock)*
I *wish* I had a horse *(Nothing happens.)*

(BILLY *and* TEDDY *do funny wake-up, then listen with greedy eyes.*)

JACK. I *want* a strong and mighty horse to help me climb up that mountain. (*Nothing happens.*)
I *need* a mighty, fiery steed, a fierce and lively horse that will help me get the baby and bring him home!!!

(BALTHAZAR, *the horse, appears. He's a silly looking, but noble, hobby horse.*)

Whoa, Balthazar! Steady, boy, steady. What a grand steed you are!! What a fine and proud dancing horse!!

(BILLY *and* TEDDY *make a great show of waking up.*)

TEDDY. That's something, that is. A grand horse like that.

BILLY. Think what we could do with that shamrock, get it in the right hands.

TEDDY. Our hands. The first wish is mine.

BILLY. No mine. I saw it first.

BILLY & TEDDY. Mine. No mine. No mine. I had the idea. I pretended to sleep first. Etc.

BILLY. We need a plan. Come here and listen.

(BILLY *and* TEDDY *huddle, as* JACK *mounts the horse and prances around.*)

BILLY. Oh, Jack. Say, Jack.

TEDDY. Hey, little brother. Nice horse you've got there. Mind if I have a look?

JACK. Not at all, Teddy. Isn't he grand? (*dismounts; leads the horse over to* TEDDY)

TEDDY. This is a grand steed. The finest I've seen. Look at that white mane. Look at those fiery eyes.

(TEDDY *goes to mount the horse, is bucked off.* BILLY *reaches around behind* JACK, *puts hand in his pocket to steal the shamrock.* BALTHAZAR *sees what's going on, nips* BILLY*'s hand.*)

BILLY. Ow ow ow ow ow!! That great beast bit my hand. I'll give him a trashing, horse or no horse.

(BALTHAZAR talks into JACK's ear. JACK nods.)

TEDDY. Is that horse talking? *(to BILLY)* I think the horse is talking. *(to JACK)* Is that a talking horse?

JACK. Well, now that you ask, yes, he does talk a bit, don't you, Balthazar? I didn't particularly ask for a talking horse and an honest horse he is. So don't go after my Golden Shamrock and be off the twose of you. I'll get the baby myself. *(exits on horseback)*

BILLY. That's all right. We don't care.

TEDDY. Yeah. We don't care. *(to BILLY)* We don't?

BILLY. No. We'll just, uh, go home to our father. That's what we'll do.

TEDDY. But, I don't want to go home. Daddy's always hollering and making fun of us.

BILLY. *(under his breath)* We're not going home I have a plan.

TEDDY. Oh, good. A plan. And then a riddle? Will you tell me a riddle? *(begins to exit)*

BILLY. Stop! We're not going there. We're going back to the Queen and her daughter

TEDDY. But she'll put us back in the dungeon. I don't like it; it's too damp and the bread doesn't taste nice.

BILLY. She won't put us in the dungeon. You'll see.

(BILLY and TEDDY trek to the door of the castle. BILLY rings the doorbell.)

QUEEN. *(enters)* Yes? My goodness me, I thought there were three of you! And where's my baby boy?

BILLY. Oh, your Royal Gracious Mightiness, we strove and we strove, the three of us, but it was no good. There was a great dragon with fire coming out of his mouth…

TEDDY. Fire. And smoke.

BILLY. And then, while we was looking the other way, our poor brother was taken by the Golden Bees and now he's all of a golden statue and there was no getting in the gate at all, so please have pity on us and let us rest a while.

QUEEN. Well, that's a sad tale, I'm sure. And I have to say I'm pleased that at the leastways two of you came back.

TEDDY. That's right. And did you ever know the difference between a goose and a duck?

QUEEN. *(Pause. Look.)* And as long as no one asks me a riddle…

BILLY. No, he won't, I swear. He won't.

QUEEN. Well, then, you're fine and welcome and my daughter Griselda will see you to your rooms and make sure you're comfortable. Griselda!!

GRISELDA. Yes Mama!

QUEEN. Show these men these their rooms. *(exits)*

(**GRISELDA** *leads them off. From offstage…*)

TEDDY. Do *you* know the difference between a goose and a duck?

(sound of a hard SLAP!!)

JACK. *(enters riding* **BALTHAZAR***)* Whoa, there! Slowly, now, slowly…

(**JACK** *and horse climbing and slipping business.*)

JACK. There it is! Whew! What a climb. But we made it.

(Other actors come out with **BEES** *to help audience make the sound of angry, buzzing, bees.)*

JACK. What's that?

(Audience takes out their **BEES** *and begins to move them around.)*

JACK. And what's that noise?

(Audience buzzes like angry bees.)

JACK. It's the Golden Bees and they're going to sting me and turn me into a golden statue and I'll be here forever. *(Pause. Thinks. Takes out Golden Shamrock).*
I wish…. *(Buzzing continues.)*
I want….. *(Buzzing continues.)*
I NEED these buzzing angry bees to stop being angry and to STOP buzzing and to let me pass so I can bring the baby back to his mother!!!!

(**BEES** *become nice bees. Actors with* **BEES** *leave.*)

JACK. Well, this Golden Shamrock's sure worth it. Now I can finally make it up the slippery golden mountain. I guess all the talk about the dragon was just that. Talk and blather.

(**JACK** *talks to* **BALTHAZAR,** *then to audience…they all agree there is no dragon…then…*)

(**DRAGON** *enters. Cardboard smoke and fire.* **BALTHA-ZAAR** *is spooked and runs off. As he leaves he knocks the Magic Shamrock out of* **JACK***'s hands.*)

JACK. *(somewhat frozen with terror)* Oh. My. Goodness. THE dragon. What Now?

LEPRECHAUN. *(appears behind him, whispers)* It's inside you, my boy. All the courage, strength and fortitude you'll ever need is right there, inside you. What is it you're always saying?

JACK. Well, I may be this and I may be that
But as sure as I'm wearing my green hat
I know I'm Irish and that's a fact
And we always go forward, we never go back!

LEPRECHAUN. That's the trick. Always go forward… *(whispering and disappearing)* forward…forward

(**JACK** *and the* **DRAGON** *fight back and forth and back and forth.* **JACK** *wins. The* **DRAGON** *slinks off.* **JACK** *is on the ground.*)

QUEEN/MINES. *(V.O.)* Arise, fair prince. You have climbed my Golden Mountain and tamed my Golden Stinging Bees and now you have slain that ghastly, annoying dragon. You are obviously a man of great worth, courage, and goodness, perhaps even a prince. And I, The Queen of the Golden Mines, salute you.

JACK. Thank you. Now please hand me the baby boy so that I can return him to his mother, for she is fearful sad and lonely…

(**BABY** *appears. [Carriage rolls in, or cradle is lowered, or…]*)

QUEEN/MINES. *(V.O.)* What are your just standing there for? Be off with you. Go. Move forward. The both of you.

  (**JACK** *exits with baby.*)

  (**BILLY** *and* **TEDDY** *enter with checkerboard. They are playing checkers with the* **QUEEN.** *They are very slow. She double-jumps them with style.*)

TEDDY. She's good…

  (**JACK** *enters with baby.* **BILLY** *and* **TEDDY** *do double take look, scream, drop checkers.*)

QUEEN. Oh, my son, my baby boy, my dear and only son. *(to* **JACK***)* You've given me back the light of my life.

JACK. Only too pleased to be able to help, your Royal Gracious Highest Majesty.

BILLY & TEDDY. Oh my goodness. Jack! Well, if it isn't Jack! We thought you were…

JACK. Never you mind what you thought. I know what you thought.

TEDDY. You see, your Majesty, it's this way, what happened was…

BILLY. No no no. It was this way. See, your Majesty, it was just that I was…

TEDDY. No, it was me was…

BILLY. Don't listen to him, it was…

QUEEN. *(holds up a hand)* SHH! *(Pause. Look.)* Dungeon!

BILLY/TEDDY. We were just on our way.

JACK. *(to* **QUEEN***)* Your Majesty, I'm proud to have brought your baby boy back, but I must tell you, I didn't do it alone. You see, there was this Wise Man I met along the way. He was the first one to help me, besides the Leprechaun, and then Balthazar, a truly noble steed, and then somehow the bees became sweet and gentle, and then the dragon, of course…I wouldn't have had the courage to take the journey to bring your baby back…or the courage to ask you…to ask you…To… ask for your daughter's hand in marriage.

  (**GRISELDA** *comes rushing out to* **JACK.** *Long hug, during which…*)

QUEEN. Griselda???!!!

GRISELDA. *(still hugging)* Yes, Mama?

QUEEN. I shall tell you, Griselda, whom you like and whom you do not like. *(Pause. Hug continues)* And, as I said, you *will* like him, Griselda.

GRISELDA. Thank you, Mama!

(Love Love, Hug Hug, Happy happy. Music up, then music under as **JACK** *breaks from hug, steps forward.)*

JACK. As in all good stories…each of us ended up right where we were supposed to be. The queen was entirely happy to be reunited with her baby boy, who grew up to be big and strong and rule The Far Country as a fair and loving King. My brothers, they ended up staying with the queen of the far country, where they actually took a liking the dungeon…

TEDDY. Did I tell you the one about he frog and the toad…?

JACK. And I…I moved back to Ireland and married Griselda where I became the first Prince and she my Princess.

QUEEN/MINES. *(V.O.)* Stop! all of you.!!!

(Music stops…All look center to the **QUEEN** *of the Golden Mines light.)*

QUEEN/MINES. *(V.O.)* I think you are forgetting something. If it wasn't for my angry bees becoming nice…Let me hear you nice bees…

*(***QUEEN/MINES*** *starts nice* **BEES** *sound, actors pick up sound, audience picks up sound. start bbbbbb audience starts bbbbbbbbbb.)*

QUEEN/MINES. *(V.O.)* Stop! If it wasn't for these nice bees here today…We wouldn't have a story now, would we???

(All actors shake heads, No.)

(Music up, actors dance in line and into special individual dances into curtain call.)

End of Play

www.ingramcontent.com/pod-product-compliance
Lightning Source LLC
Chambersburg PA
CBHW070423120726